It's not JUST a blanket!

Written and illustrated by

ANNALIESE STONEY

BONNEY PRESS

Published by Bonney Press,
an imprint of Hinkler Books Pty Ltd
45–55 Fairchild Street
Heatherton Victoria 3202 Australia
www.hinkler.com.au

BONNEY
PRESS

©Hinkler Books Pty Ltd 2014, 2015

Author and illustrator: Annaliese Stoney

ISBN: 978 1 7436 7795 7

Printed and bound in China

For Steve and my family, for all their cheerleading!

It's not **JUST** a blanket...

Sophia *loved* her blanket **VERY** much.

Everywhere...

and

ANYWHERE

that she and her dog Monty went,

the blanket came too!

Her family didn't understand why.

they said.

But Sophia knew better.

MUNCH
MUNCH

It's not JUST a blanket!
It's a...

Slippery stingray!

It's not JUST a blanket! It's a...

It's not JUST a blanket! Look! It's a...

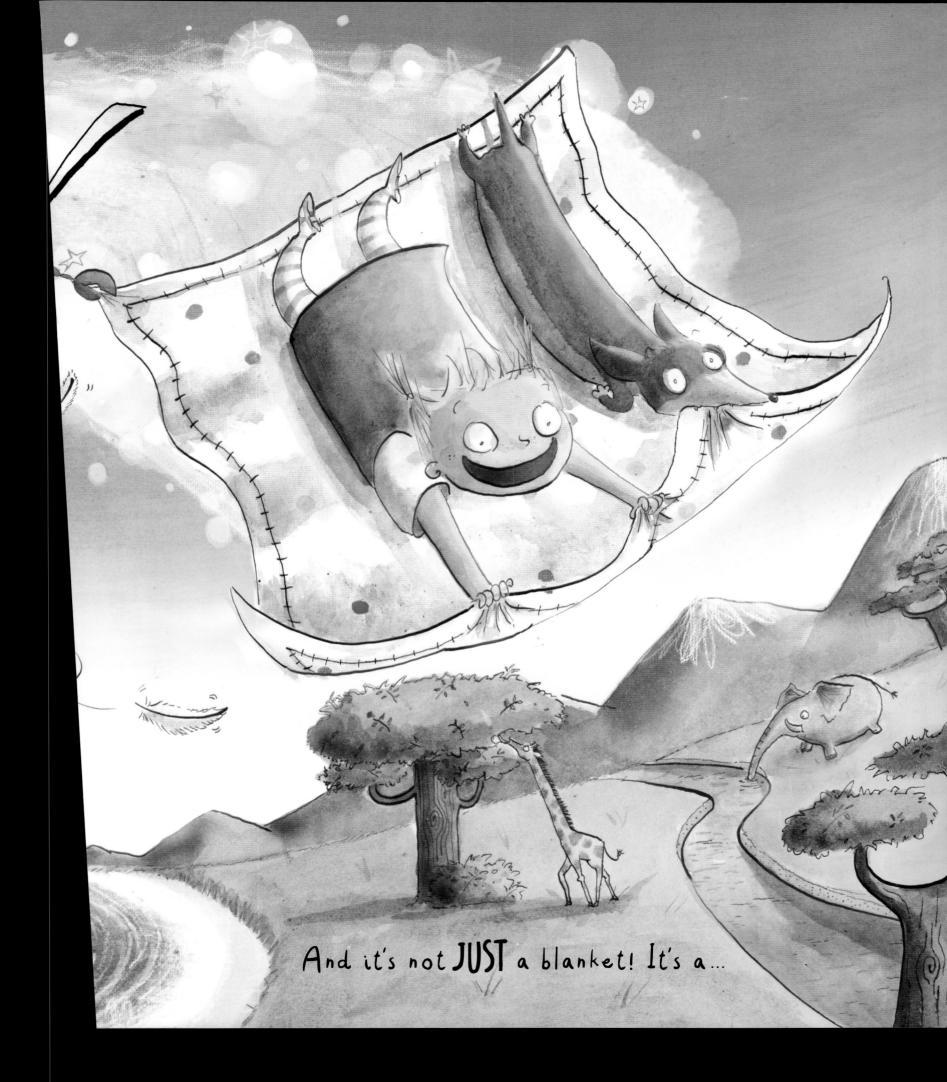

And it's not JUST a blanket! It's a...

And it's not JUST a blanket! It's a...

Poor Sophia was very upset.

Monty felt pretty bad, too.

Her brother Clive saw the whole thing.

He told the whole family,

who thought very hard, until eventually they came up with

A BRILLIANT PLAN...

$mc^2 = \frac{1}{4}$

First, Dad collected all the torn bits of blanket.

Clive took off his starry socks.

Grandma found an old pair of bloomers,

and Mum generously donated Dad's Hawaiian shirt collection.

Then, armed with a big bundle of material, they worked very, very hard, until...

GASP!

"TA-DA!" they exclaimed.
"Here you are Sophia and Monty. We know how much you loved that old blanket, so we've made you BOTH new blankets."

"Thank you very much!" Sophia and Monty said.

"The only thing is...

not JUST blankets!"